The Tale of Despereaux™

Glow-in-the-Dark
Sticker Book

Based on the motion picture screenplay
Based on the book by Kate DiCamillo

CANDLEWICK PRESS

The Royal Kitchen

The Kingdom of Dor is known far and wide for its amazing, wonderful soup.
Each year André, the royal chef, creates a new recipe, which is presented on
Royal Soup Day. Sometimes he even gets a little magical help!

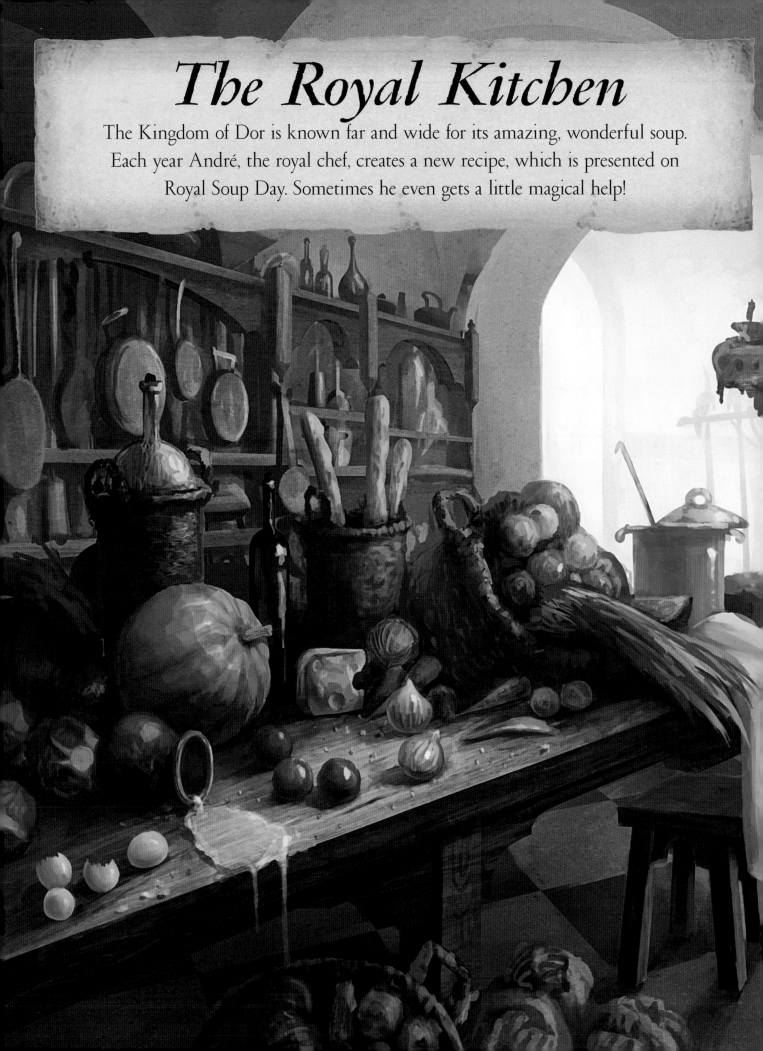

The Mouse World

Deep within the castle walls, there is a miniature world where Despereaux and his family live with all the other mice. Despereaux may be small, but he is very, very brave. He can spring a mousetrap faster than you can say "cheese!"

Royal Kitchen Stickers

Dungeon Stickers

Pea's Chamber Stickers

Mouse World Stickers

The Dungeon

In the depths of the castle is the dungeon, home to the bones of unlucky prisoners . . . and to the rats. Led by Botticelli, the rats revel in the shadows and glory in the dark filth of the rat world. All except for one rat, Roscuro, who misses the light he loves.

Pea's Chamber

Princess Pea has servants, lovely clothes, and a jeweled tiara, but she is sad and lonely. Often she stares longingly out her window at the gray sky. Then one day a very small gentleman comes to visit, and everything changes.